This SCRIBBLERS
book belongs to:

................................

FOR ALL CAT LOVERS – J.H.D

This edition published in Great Britain in MMXX
by Scribblers, an imprint of
The Salariya Book Company Ltd
25 Marlborough Place,
Brighton BN1 1UB
www.salariya.com

Text © Joy H. Davidson MMXVIII
Illustrations © Jenny Cooper MMXVIII
English language © The Salariya Book Company Ltd MMXX
First published in New Zealand by DHD Publishing Ltd
Original title: OH NO! Look what the cat dragged in

HB ISBN-13: 978-1-912904-60-0

1 3 5 7 9 8 6 4 2

A CIP catalogue record for this book is
available from the British Library.

Printed and bound in China

Printed on paper from sustainable sources

Visit
www.salariya.com
for our online catalogue and
**free** fun stuff.

# Oh No! Look What The Cat Dragged In

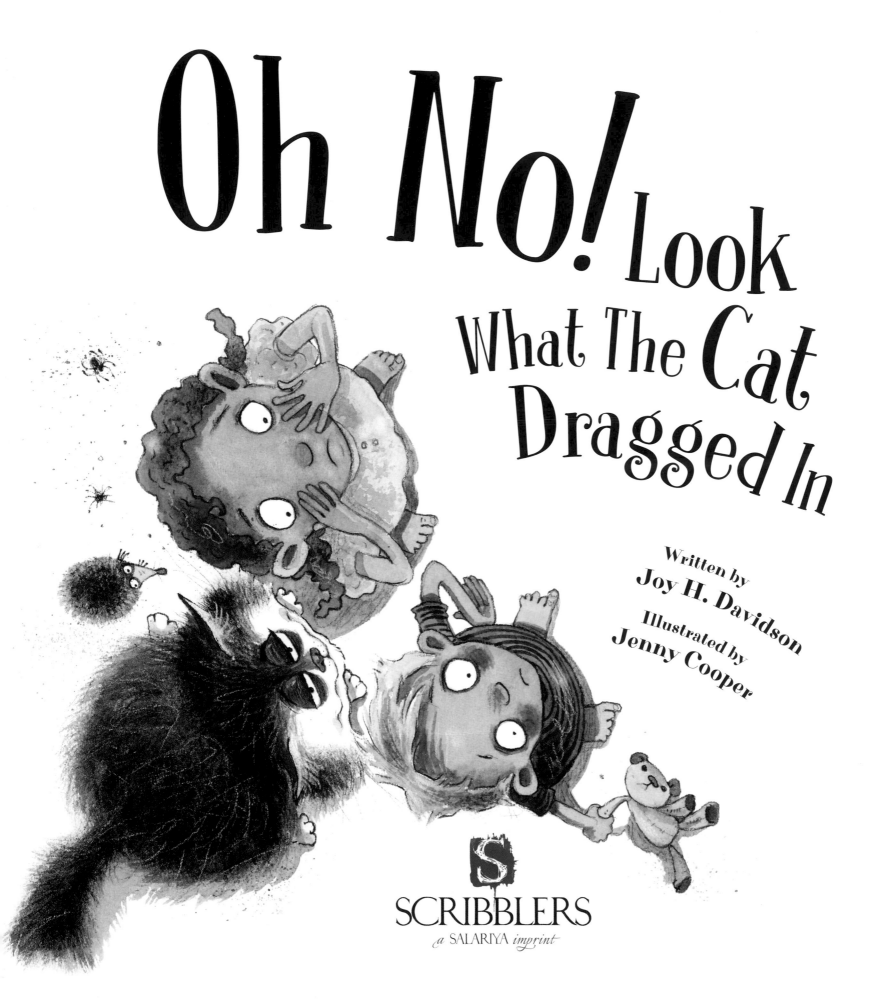

Written by
**Joy H. Davidson**

Illustrated by
**Jenny Cooper**

**SCRIBBLERS**
*a* SALARIYA *imprint*

We like to stay with Grandma, but she has a big black cat. He likes to go out late at night, and he drags things through the flap.

But Grandma's acting worried,
and looking very grim.
She never knows each morning just WHAT the cat dragged in.

When we woke up on Monday,
got dressed and skipped downstairs,
we found our anxious grandma,
**standing on a chair.**
She was pointing at the kitchen,
and looking **very grim.**

'OH NO!' she cried.

'Look what the **CAT** dragged in.'

Lots of creepy crawlies were climbing up the wall,
while a very prickly hedgehog was running down the hall.
An enormous smelly rat was lying on the rug,
and a big brown shiny cockroach was crawling up the jug.

When we woke up on Tuesday,
got dressed and ran downstairs,
we found our troubled grandma tearing out her hair.
She was pointing at the kitchen and looking very grim.

Small grey mice and lizards were scurrying all around,
and an army of busy ants were marching up and down.
A strange pair of underwear were lying on the floor,
and a large hairy bat was hanging on the kitchen door.

When we woke up on Wednesday,
got dressed and walked downstairs,
we found our weepy grandma bursting into tears.
She was pointing at the kitchen and looking very grim.

'OH NO NO NO!' she cried.

'Look what the CAT dragged in.'

A gruesome hairy spider was sitting on the tap,
And a slinky hissing green snake was coiled up on the mat.
There were big fat juicy maggots eyeing up the bin,
While two giant grasshoppers tap-danced on a tin.

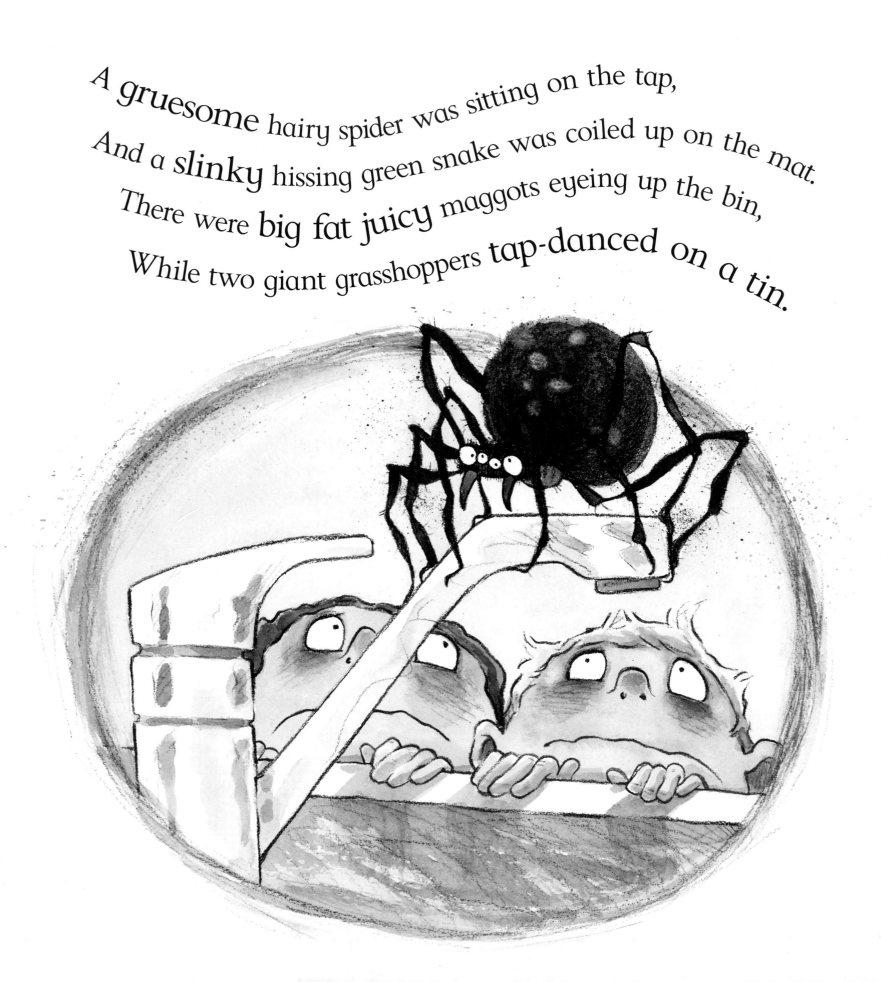

When we woke up on Thursday,
got dressed and sneaked downstairs,
we found our worried grandma hanging from the chandelier.
She was pointing at the kitchen and looking very grim.

'OH NO NO NO NO!' she cried. 'Look what the CAT dragged in.'

Two birds under the kitchen chair,
were pretending very hard to look dead,
and lots more scary creatures were buzzing
  around our heads.
A rather angry weasel was snarling at the cat,
and someone's dirty laundry was strewn
  across the mat!

When we woke up on Friday,
got dressed and crept downstairs,
we found our horrified grandma,
looking really scared.
She was pointing at the kitchen and looking very grim.

'OH NO NO NO NO NO!' she cried.
'Look what the CAT dragged in.'

There were creepy crawlies everywhere and garbage
  piled up high.
The cat was in his basket, keeping a watchful eye.
The garbage was very smelly now and all the creatures
  ran amuck.
I don't know how we'll clean it up.
We'll have to hire a truck.

When we woke up on Saturday we hid ourselves upstairs,
it was far too terrifying to venture down the stairs.

We could hear all kinds of noises - it was pandemonium!

Grandma was loudly grumbling about what the CAT had done.

When we woke up on Sunday,

we peeked cautiously downstairs,

and to our astonishment...

our grandma wasn't there.

We found her in the kitchen,
as calm as calm could be.
She was cooking us
some breakfast,
and brewing up some tea.

We looked around the kitchen.
We couldn't believe the view.
Everything was spotlessly clean.
It shone and smelled like new.

The cat was asleep in his basket,
and loudly snoring away.
Our grandma had been busy,

she'd really saved the day!

She'd **nailed up** the cat flap,
and **locked** the windows tight.
She told us,

'Now, in the future, that CAT stays in at night!'